NO BOWS!

Written by Shirley Smith Duke

Illustrated by Jenny Mattheson

PEACHTREE
ATLANTA

To D. L. D. and M. J. D.

—*S. S. D.*

For my parents

—*J. M.*

Published by
PEACHTREE PUBLISHERS
1700 Chattahoochee Avenue
Atlanta, Georgia 30318-2112

www.peachtree-online.com

Text © 2006 by Shirley Smith Duke
Illustrations © 2006 by Jenny Mattheson

Book design by Jenny Mattheson and Loraine M. Joyner
Illustrations created in oil on primed 100% rag archival paper
Title and text typeset in Monotype's Century Gothic

Printed and manufactured in Singapore
10 9 8 7 6 5 4 3 2 1
First Edition

ISBN 1-56145-356-0

Library of Congress Cataloging-in-Publication Data

Duke, Shirley Smith.
  No bows! / written by Shirley Smith Duke ; illustrated by Jenny Mattheson.-- 1st
ed.
      p. cm.
  Summary: A toddler expresses her opinions on what to wear, eat, and play, but
there is one thing she will accept without argument.

  ISBN 1-56145-356-0
  [1. Toddlers--Fiction.] I. Mattheson, Jenny, ill. II. Title.
  PZ7.D88944No 2006
  [E]--dc22
                              2005020029

no bows...

BRAIDS

no pink...

PURPLE

no puppy...

LIZARD

no piano...

DRUMS

no dress...

DRESS-UP

no shoes...

no sandbox...

MUD

no nap...

STORY

The King knew he could not defeat the fiery dragon alone.

Just in time the brave Princess galloped up, swinging her shining sword.

no park...

no vanilla...

no crayons...

no soap...

no bunny...

BEAR

no night-light...

Hugs?